This book belongs to

Chelsea

. . . .

For Florrie Lawrie
because she's so sweet

A JAR
FULL OF MICE

by

Diz Wallis

CAROLINE HOUSE

There was once a house that was full of mice. There were mice everywhere. They had lived there for years completely at peace—until the day the new cook came. Cook made puddings as light as feathers, and her services were highly prized; so when she said, "I cannot abide a house with a mouse," action was taken.

"Madam," she said, "it's the mice or me. We must get a cat and straight away, for I just cannot stand those scampers and squeaks, those quivery whiskers and tails that twitch."

So her mistress went off in search of a cat. She soon fell in love with a Persian queen called Jasmine, who had a soft, silky coat and amber eyes that opened wide with surprise when she heard the word "work!" For she was far too well bred for that. She was furry and purry, but she couldn't catch mice. And she also had very expensive tastes. Cook did not approve.

"What we need is a proper cat. I shall find one for you."

So a second cat was acquired. It was a tabby cat, a shabby cat with a broken tail and a tattered ear; an alley cat who had other things on his mind aside from hunting mice. Every night he would let himself out by the back door and go dancing and singing in the moonlight. Then he would have to sleep, sleep, sleep all day long. Cook was disgusted.

"What we need is a GOOD MOUSER," she said.

Very soon a third cat arrived. It was bouncing about in a wicker basket with a lid that was tied down tightly and bore a label with the words "GOOD MOUSER" written on it. When Cook undid the string, out flew the cat. It moved so fast you couldn't tell what color it was. It went straight to work, for this was a cat who loved a chase. Cook was delighted, and she smiled a smile that was not quite nice—for she just couldn't bear mice, she couldn't abide them, she felt no sympathy at all.

Poor little mice! They had nowhere to run—the cat was always right behind. At last it chased them into the larder—up the shelves, down the shelves—they ran round and round till packets toppled and jars were broken. They were in trouble, for there was no place to hide—till one mouse spotted an open jar and they jumped inside. Somebody had left the top off! The jar was blue and white and had come all the way from China, full of ginger. Now it was almost empty, and, one after the other, quick as a flash, into the sticky jar they dropped, making no sound at all.

They disappeared so suddenly that the cat was confused and shook its head. It waited; it listened. The silence was total. The tiniest noise would have betrayed them, but no sound came from the open jar. The stillness in the pantry was deep, so deep you could have heard a whisker twitch. Then someone sneezed the teeniest sneeze, the teeniest, tiniest, weeniest sneeze, and the cat was upon them. It thrust its paw down into the shadow beneath the blue rim of the porcelain jar just at the moment when Cook came into the pantry.

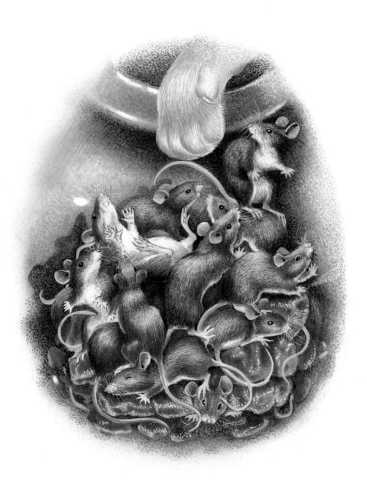

She was about to make one of her famous puddings. "Puss!" she screamed. "You get your paw out of my ginger!" And she put back the lid without looking inside. Then she saw the state of the pantry and she sent the cat packing with a flea in its ear—it had gone too far. She muttered and mumbled, she groaned and she grumbled about the mess and the waste and the cost of things. What kind of pudding could she cook now that the ingredients were scattered across the floor? Ginger pudding, of course. The jar felt full—"Plenty of ginger in this," she said.

Back in the kitchen the maids had assembled to watch the mixing of the marvelous pud. "Now, girls," Cook said, "this is of the utmost importance. Only the best of ingredients will do—like this ginger, for instance." She shook the jar and lifted the lid and tipped the contents towards the bowl. Then—Oh! Pandemonium! What a disaster! Such screams, such shrieks you never have heard. Out of the jar and onto the table tumbled the squeaking, squealing mice.

Cook was appalled. She dropped the jar and ran from the kitchen, her face aflame. She ran and she ran, and she never returned, for she couldn't abide a house with a mouse. As for the mice, they were quite happy, for peace had returned. Cook and Good Mouser were gone forever, whilst Tabby Cat, Shabby Cat danced and slept, and Jasmine ate ginger and purred all day.

And what of the jar? That was taken out to the garden shed to be mended one day. It stood on a shelf in a dark, dusty corner, where the air was musty and spiders played. It stayed there for years and years, till the timbers rotted and the little shed crumbled away to dust.

Perhaps the pieces are still there somewhere, hidden in the tangled grass.